Firefighters!

Speeding! Spraying! Saving!

written by
Patricia Hubbell

illustrated by
Viviana Garofoli

Marshall Cavendish Children

To Sergio for his love and cooperation—V.G.

Marshall Cavendish Corporation, 99 White Plains Road, Tarrytown, NY 10591
www.marshallcavendish.us

Library of Congress Cataloging-in-Publication Data

Hubbell, Patricia.
Firefighters! : speeding! spraying! saving! / by Patricia Hubbell ; illustrations by Viviana Garofoli.
p. cm.
Summary: Illustrations and rhyming text celebrate firefighters and what they do.
ISBN-13: 978-0-7614-5337-6 (alk. paper)
[1. Fire fighters–Fiction. 2. Stories in rhyme.] I. Garófoli, Viviana, ill. II. Title.

PZ8.3.H848Fir 2006
[E]–dc22

2006012989

The text of this book is set in Futura Heavy.
The illustrations are rendered in Adobe Illustrator.
Book design by Vera Soki

Printed in China
First edition
1 3 5 6 4 2

mc Marshall Cavendish
Children

CLANG! CLANG! CLANG!

Firefighters rush! Scurry!
Down the pole. Slide! Hurry!

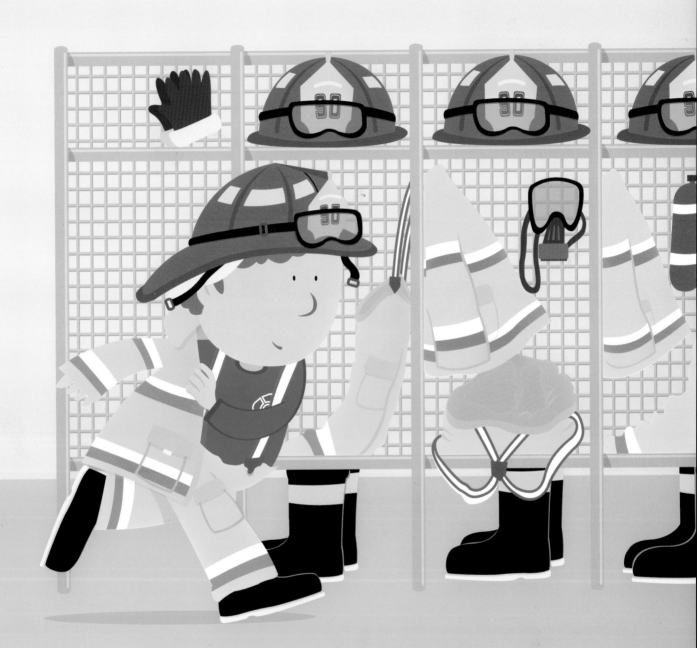

Put on great big fireproof suits.
Put on helmets, gloves, and boots.

Here comes Spot, the pet Dalmatian,

ready to leave the fire station.

Swing aboard! Hit the gas.

Ladder truck roars, heads out fast.

Sirens screech—Whee-ahh! Whooo!

HHHH!!! WHOOOOOOO!

Pumper truck comes zooming through!

Chief's car races, warning lights flash.

WHEE-AHH! WHEE-AHH! WHEE-AHH! WHOOO!

Cars pull over, engines pass.

Lift the ladders, haul the hose.

Hydrant's open, water flows.

Flames flare up into the sky.

Aim that water, shoot it high.

Crackle! Sizzle! Thunder! Roar!
Swing that hatchet, break the door.

Firefighter starts to shout,
"There may be people to get out."

Raise the platform! Bring them down!

Safe and sound
on solid ground.

Hooray! Hooray! Watchers cheer.

Rescue truck is waiting near.

Grab the saws, axes, sledges.
To the roof, walls, and ledges.

Water whooshes, hisses, sprays.
Fire crew has saved the day.

No more danger. Fire's out.
Only ashes swirl about.

Pack the trucks, coil the hose.

Back to town the tired crew goes.

Check equipment, clean each truck.

Clean the clothes of guck and muck.

Rest. Talk. Laugh. Eat.
Spot gets a special treat.

All is quiet. All is still.
Firefighters relax until . . .